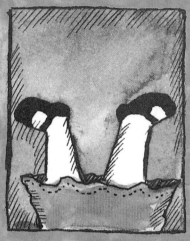

THE
MISS NELSON
COLLECTION

www.hmhco.com

ISBN: 978-0-544-08222-9

Manufactured in China
SCP 10 9 8 7 6 5
4500610602

THE MISS NELSON COLLECTION

Harry Allard

James Marshall

Houghton Mifflin Harcourt
Boston   New York

CONTENTS

MISS NELSON IS MISSING!
HARRY ALLARD
JAMES MARSHALL

The kids in Room 207 were misbehaving again.

Spitballs stuck to the ceiling.

Paper planes whizzed through the air.

They were the worst-behaved class in the whole school.

"Now settle down," said Miss Nelson in a sweet voice.

But the class would *not* settle down.

They whispered and giggled.

They squirmed and made faces.

They were even rude during story hour.

And they always refused to do their lessons.

"Something will have to be done," said Miss Nelson.

The next morning Miss Nelson did not come to school.
"Wow!" yelled the kids. "Now we can *really* act up!"
They began to make more spitballs and paper planes.
"Today let's be just terrible!" they said.

"Not so fast!" hissed an unpleasant voice.

  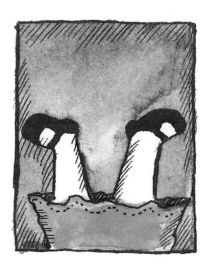

A woman in an ugly black dress stood before them.

"I am your new teacher, Miss Viola Swamp."

And she rapped the desk with her ruler.

"Where is Miss Nelson?" asked the kids.

"Never mind that!" snapped Miss Swamp. "Open those arithmetic books!"

Miss Nelson's kids did as they were told.

They could see that Miss Swamp was a real witch.

She meant business.

Right away she put them to work.

And she loaded them down with homework.

"We'll have no story hour today," said Miss Swamp.
"Keep your mouths shut," said Miss Swamp.
"Sit perfectly still," said Miss Swamp.
"And if you misbehave, you'll be sorry," said
Miss Swamp.

The kids in Room 207 had *never* worked so hard.

Days went by and there was no sign of Miss Nelson.
The kids *missed* Miss Nelson!

"Maybe we should try to find her," they said.
Some of them went to the police.

Detective McSmogg was assigned to the case.
He listened to their story.
He scratched his chin.
"Hmmmm," he said. "Hmmm."
"I think Miss Nelson is missing."
Detective McSmogg would
not be much help.

Other kids went to Miss Nelson's house.

The shades were tightly drawn, and no one answered the door.

In fact, the only person they *did* see was the wicked Miss Viola Swamp, coming up the street.

"If she sees us, she'll give us more homework."

They got away just in time.

Maybe something *terrible* happened to Miss Nelson!
"Maybe she was gobbled up by a shark!" said one of the kids.
But that didn't seem likely.

SHARKS
(VERY UNPLEASANT)

"Maybe Miss Nelson went to Mars!" said another kid.
But that didn't seem likely either.

"I know!" exclaimed one know-it-all. "Maybe Miss Nelson's
car was carried off by a swarm of angry butterflies!"
But that was the least likely of all.

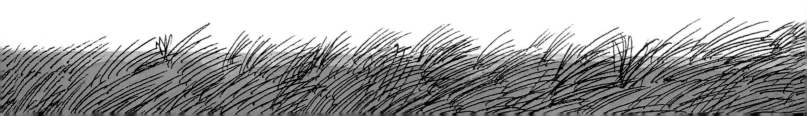

The kids in Room 207 became very discouraged.

It seemed that Miss Nelson was never coming back.

And they would be stuck with Miss Viola Swamp forever.

They heard footsteps in the hall.

"Here comes the witch," they whispered.

"Hello, children," someone said in a sweet voice.

It was Miss Nelson!

"Did you miss me?" she asked.

"We certainly did!" cried all the kids.

"Where were you?"

"That's my little secret," said Miss Nelson.

"How about a story hour?"

"Oh yes!" cried the kids.

Miss Nelson noticed that during story hour no one
was rude or silly.

"What brought about this lovely change?" she asked.

"That's *our* little secret," said the kids.

Back home Miss Nelson took off her coat and hung it
in the closet (right next to an ugly black dress).
When it was time for bed she sang a little song.
"I'll never tell," she said to herself with a smile.

P.S. Detective McSmogg is working on a new case.
He is *now* looking for Miss Viola Swamp.

MISS NELSON IS BACK

HARRY ALLARD

JAMES MARSHALL

For Miss Audrey Bruce

One Friday Miss Nelson told her class that
she was going to have her tonsils out.
"I'll be away next week," she said.
"And I expect you to behave."
"Yes, Miss Nelson," said the kids in 207.

But at recess it was another story.
"Wow!" said the kids. "While Miss Nelson is away,
we can really act up!"
"Not so fast!" said a big kid from 309.
"Haven't you ever heard of Viola Swamp?"

"Who?" said Miss Nelson's kids.

"Miss Swamp is the meanest substitute
in the whole world," said the big kid.
"Nobody acts up when she's around."
"Oooh," said Miss Nelson's kids.
"She's a real witch," said the big kid.
"Oooh," said Miss Nelson's kids.

"I'll just bet you get the Swamp!" said the big kid.

On Monday morning Miss Nelson's kids were all
in their seats.
They were very nervous.
Some of them had not slept well all weekend.

"If we get the Swamp, I'll just die," said one kid.
They heard footsteps in the hall.

Slowly the knob turned.

And the door opened . . .

It was Mr. Blandsworth, the principal.

"I shall personally take over this class," he said.

Miss Nelson's kids were *so* relieved.

But they soon learned that Mr. Blandsworth
was not a lot of fun.

All morning Mr. Blandsworth tried to amuse the class
with his corny card tricks.

"Oh, brother," said the class.

That afternoon Mr. Blandsworth showed the class
his favorite shadow pictures.

"This is kids' stuff," said the class.

The next day Mr. Blandsworth demonstrated
his favorite bird calls.
They were not a success.

And for two days Mr. Blandsworth showed slides
of his goldfish Lucille.
Miss Nelson's kids had never been so bored.

While dusting erasers in the schoolyard,
three of the ringleaders of 207 discussed the situation.
"Something will have to be done," they said.
"We must get rid of Blandsworth."

And they hatched a plot.

After school they painted and sewed
and borrowed some old clothes.

And they practiced some very difficult
stunt work in the back yard.

The next day they weren't in class.
"That's too bad," said Mr. Blandsworth.
"They'll miss all the excitement."

Mr. Blandsworth was about to show the class
his collection of ballpoint pens
from all over the world,
when someone came to the door.

Slowly the knob turned.

And the door opened . . .

"Oh, look!" said the class. "Miss Nelson is back!"

A tall and lumpy Miss Nelson tottered into the room.

Mr. Blandsworth was surprised.

"You're back sooner than we expected," he said.

The tall and lumpy Miss Nelson didn't speak.

"Er," said the kids. "Her throat must still be sore."

"Are you sure you're well enough?" said Mr. Blandsworth.

"She's sure," said the kids.

"Well, in that case," said the principal, "I'll be getting back to the office. Nice to have you back, Miss Nelson." And he left the room.

"Hot dog!" cried the class.
"We got rid of Blandsworth!
Now we can do just as we please!"

And at the stroke of ten, the kids from 207
left the building.
No one stopped them.

They went straight to the movies, where they saw
The Monster That Ate Chicago—twice.
"This is really living," they said.

Afterward they went to Lulu's, where
they stuffed themselves silly.
But soon they made a serious mistake.

Heading back to school, they passed Miss Nelson's house.

Miss Nelson couldn't believe her eyes.

"Those are my kids!" she said in a scratchy voice.

"What are they doing out of school?

And who is that with them?"

Miss Nelson telephoned
Mr. Blandsworth to see
what was going on.

"You're not Miss Nelson,"
said Blandsworth.
"Miss Nelson is back."

And he hung up.
"Can't fool me," he said.
"Hmm," said Miss Nelson.
"Something will have
to be done."
And she went to her closet.

Back in 207 Miss Nelson's kids were spending
an agreeable afternoon.

They were very pleased with themselves.
"We should do this more often," they said.
They did not notice the figure out in the hall.

Slowly the knob turned.

And the door opened . . .

"My name is Viola Swamp," said the lady in a scratchy voice.

"Yipes!" cried the kids. "The Swamp!"

"That's right!" said Miss Swamp.
"And I'm here to whip this class into shape.
 Get back to those desks on the double!"

The class did as it was told.
The big kid from 309 was certainly right—
Miss Swamp was a real witch!

She knew how to get results.

The class did a whole week's work in no time.

"We shouldn't have gotten rid of Blandsworth," they said.

"Pipe down!" said the Swamp, "or . . ."
Just then something under a desk
attracted her attention.

It was a mask.

"Ah ha!" said Miss Swamp. "So *that's* your little game!"
And she tried on the mask—just as Mr. Blandsworth
stepped into the room.

"Miss Nelson," said Blandsworth. "I'm of the opinion that
someone has been impersonating you."

"Uh oh," whispered the kids.

"You don't say," said Miss Swamp.
"Probably just some kids acting up.
I'm *sure* it won't happen again."
And Mr. Blandsworth left.

"And it won't, will it?" said Miss Swamp to the class.

"Because the Swamp will be watching!"

A minute later, Miss Nelson appeared.

"I'm back," she said.

"Hot dog!" cried the kids. "Are we glad to see you!"
"Didn't you have fun with Mr. Blandsworth?" asked Miss Nelson.
"Er," said the kids.

They decided not to mention Miss Viola Swamp.
But they wondered why Miss Nelson hadn't seen her in the hall.

For my godchild Charlotte Kavanagh   —H.A.
For Jack Kearney   —J.M.

For some weeks now, gloom had blanketed
the Horace B. Smedley School.
No one laughed or threw spitballs.
No one even smiled.
Miss Nelson was worried.

Everyone was down in the dumps.

Even the cafeteria ladies had lost their sparkle.

Mr. Blandsworth was so depressed he hid under his desk.

"It's the worst team in the whole state," he said.

And it was true—the Smedley Tornadoes were just pitiful.

They hadn't won a game all year.

They hadn't scored even a single point.

And lately they seemed only interested in horsing around
and in giving Coach the business.
"Why practice?" they said. "We'll only lose anyway."

"We're in for it now," said old Pop Hanson, the janitor.
"The big Thanksgiving game is coming up,
 and the Werewolves from Central are real animals.
They'll make mincemeat out of our team."
"What's to be done?" said Miss Nelson.
"We need a real expert," said Pop.

That afternoon, while Miss Nelson was grading papers, she heard wild laughter.

It was coming from the teachers' lounge.

Coach Armstrong had cracked up.

"I'll make us a fresh pot of coffee," said Miss Nelson.

When Coach had calmed down,
Miss Nelson took him home in a taxi.
"You need a nice long rest," she said.

The next day it was announced over the PA
that Coach Armstrong would
be out for a long time with the measles.
"Who will take his place?" said the kids.

When Miss Nelson passed by Lulu's after school,
a serious discussion was going on.
"We need someone who can really get the team into shape
for the big Thanksgiving game," said one kid.
"Someone who knows how to get results."
"It's too bad Miss Viola Swamp isn't around," said another.
"Who?" said a kid who was new in town.
"You've never heard of Viola Swamp?" said the first kid.
"The meanest substitute in the whole wide world?
She's a real witch. She'd have no trouble getting results."
Mr. Blandsworth happened to overhear.
"Hmmm," he said.

"Hmmm," said Miss Nelson.

And she wasted no time getting home.

After rummaging around in her closet, she found

what she was looking for—an ugly black sweat suit.

Then she made an important phone call.

"I'll be right there,"

said the voice at the other end.

The next day Mr. Blandsworth announced
that there would be football practice as usual.
"Whoever it is," said the guys, "let's really give him the business."

The doors to Coach's office flew open and out stepped . . .

a lady in an ugly black dress . . .

"My name is Viola Swamp," said the lady.
"And I am here to get results."

"It's Blandsworth!" cried the guys.
And they laughed him off the field.

"Oh, rats," said Blandsworth. "How could they tell?"
Just then the guys heard the sound of squeaky tennis shoes.

"I am Coach Swamp!" said the lady in the black sweat suit.

"Holy smoke!" cried the team. "The Swamp!"

The team's fullback tried to pussyfoot away.
"Not so fast, Mr. Smarty!" said Coach Swamp.

"Wow!" said one of the guys. "Did you see that tackle?"

Coach Swamp was a real expert.
She put the team to work right away.

The guys had never done so many leg raises.
"More!" said Coach Swamp.

They had never run so fast.
"Faster!" yelled Coach Swamp.

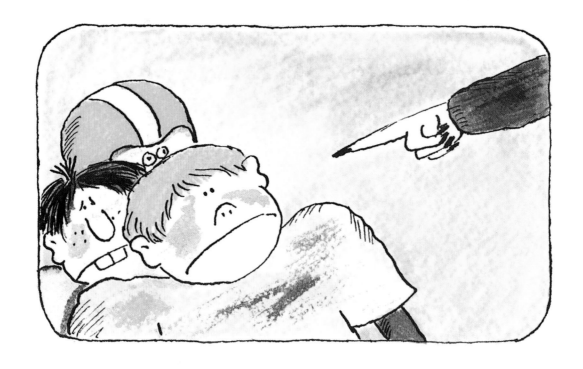

"This is murder," said the guys.
"Pipe down," said Coach Swamp.

In only a matter of days, the Smedley Tornadoes were looking better.

Coach Swamp really gave them the business.

Mr. Blandsworth was a little puzzled, however.

"Who *is* that Miss Swamp?" he said.
"Maybe Miss Nelson knows. I'll go ask."

Miss Nelson was busy grading papers when Blandsworth looked in.

"I don't want to disturb her," said Blandsworth. "She probably doesn't know, anyway."

Down on the field, Coach Swamp was having a little talk with the team.

"And don't ever think you can horse around again," she said.
"Because the Swamp will be watching!"

When Coach Armstrong returned after his rest,
he was very surprised by what he found.
The guys played like a real team.
"How did this happen?" said Coach Armstrong.

"Er," said the guys.

On Thanksgiving Day the Tornadoes clobbered the Werewolves seventy-seven to three.
It was a great day for Horace B. Smedley School.

Mr. Blandsworth treated the whole team to hot dogs at Lulu's.
Miss Nelson went home tired and happy.

"Sometimes you just have to get tough,"
she told her sister Barbara.
"And by the way, thanks for filling in for me."
"Any time," said Barbara. "Any time."